THE LONG LOST SECRET DIARY OF THE WORLD'S WORST HOLLYWOOD DIRECTOR

SCRIBO

a SALARIYA *imprint*

First published in Great Britain by Scribo MMXX
Scribo, an imprint of
The Salariya Book Company
25 Marlborough Place, Brighton, BN1 1UB

ISBN 978-1-912904-66-2

The right of Tim Collins to be identified as the author of this work has
been asserted in accordance with sections 77 and 78 of the Copyright,
Designs and Patents Act, 1988.

Book design by David Salariya

Printed and bound in China

The text for this book is set in Century Schoolbook
The display type is Jacob Riley

www.salariya.com

THE LONG-LOST SECRET DIARY OF THE WORLD'S WORST HOLLYWOOD DIRECTOR

Written by
Tim Collins

Illustrated by
Isobel Lundie

SCRIBO
a SALARIYA *imprint*

Chapter I
—

Los Angeles, 1915

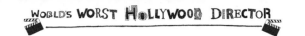

Monday 3rd May

Okay, my pulse has slowed a little now. I've finally admitted that the cops aren't coming for me. I should never have sneaked into the movie theatre, and I'll never do it again. It just seemed like such a good chance to finally see a moving picture.

Every day I go to the nickelodeons around Broadway and read the list of movies playing. Today I went to the one near 5th Street. On one side, there's a jewellery shop with fancy necklaces and bracelets. On the other there's a clothes shop with lacy white dresses and big hats. But it's the storefront in the middle you look at.

The words 'Picture Palace 5c' are written in lights above thick white pillars and a square ticket office. At the front there's a board with movies listed on it:

I never have the money to go in, and Dad is being really grouchy about money right now so there's no point asking him for some. So instead

I stand outside and imagine what happens in the movies.

Today I thought up a story for *Test of the Telephone Girl* in which a robber invades the house of a rich lady talking to a telephone operator. Then there is a crazy race against time, with the telephone girl rushing on her bicycle to the house of the rich lady, narrowly missing speeding cars and trains.

The imaginary movie finished playing in my head and I looked around and saw there was no one in the ticket office. Maybe things were so quiet in the middle of the day that the ticket girl had decided to take some time out?

'Just go in, Clara,' said a little voice in my head. It's not exactly stealing, because there are empty seats inside and the theatre will make the same money whether you stay out or go in.

Another voice told me it was wrong and I should go back to our apartment. But it was too late. I was already shoving the door open.

Inside was a hot and smoky room with about twenty rows of chairs lined up to face the wall with the movie on.

I sat in the back row and slunk down so no one could see me. I tried to enjoy the movies, but I couldn't stop feeling guilty about sneaking in. Plus, they were showing a newsreel about the war in Europe, so it wasn't exactly relaxing.

Finally, the newsreel finished. The title card for *Test of the Telephone Girl* came on, and a woman at the front started playing the piano in time with the pictures.

A bright white light shone into my eyes.

It was the girl from the booth, pointing her torch in my face.

'Where's your ticket?' she asked. 'I didn't see you come in.'

I bolted along the aisle and out the door on the other side. The ticket girl followed me and yelled something about cops.

She was probably threatening to fetch them if she ever saw me again, but in my terrified state I thought she was saying they were already on their way.

As I ran down Broadway, weaving my way around busy office clerks and old guys with grocery bags, I convinced myself that a gang of cops were on my tail and I needed to shake them off.

I kept thinking about what could happen if it were a movie. I could lean a tall ladder against a fence and use it to seesaw to the other side.

Or I could leap onto a speeding automobile and wave goodbye to the cops as they threw their hats to the ground and stamped on them in frustration.

Or I could tip over a huge cart of fresh manure and let them skid into it.

I raced all the way back to our apartment, ran into my room and hid under my blankets. I can see now that the cops were never really coming. I'd just been playing out movies in my head again and became a little carried away.

But it's fine. I got away with it, and I'll never try it again.

1

I could lean a tall ladder against a fence and use it to seesaw to the other side.

2

Or I could leap onto a speeding automobile.

3

Or I could tip over a huge cart of fresh manure and let them skid into it.

GET REAL

*People watched early movies in small
theatres known as 'nickelodeons' in the
USA. They were often set up in storefronts
where five cents was charged for
admission. They typically showed a bill of
short films that lasted around ten or fifteen
minutes each. Films had no sound in this
era, so a piano or organ would be played
live to accompany them.*

Tuesday 4ᵗʰ May

I went back to the nickelodeon to read through
the bill of movies today. I was still desperate
to see them, but there was no way I'd risk
sneaking in again.

The exit door swung open and a man in a black
jacket stepped out. As he walked down the

pavement he took a lighter out of his pocket and I heard a faint metal clink. I edged over and saw he'd accidentally dropped a shiny nickel on the floor.

I placed my shoe over the coin and made a deal with myself. If the man hadn't noticed it was gone by the time he was out of sight, I'd grab it and I wouldn't feel bad.

Soon the man was lost in the crowd and I scooped up the nickel. I recognised the girl in the booth as the one who'd chased me out of the nickelodeon yesterday, so I pushed my hair down over my face and asked for a ticket in a really deep voice.

The girl asked if I was feeling ill, and if I shouldn't go and lie down instead. I insisted on handing over my nickel, and I noticed that she wiped her hand on her sleeve after touching it like she was going to catch whatever disease that I had.

I grabbed my ticket and went in. It turns out going to the movies is much more fun when you don't have to worry about someone catching you and hauling you off to jail.

There was a chase story about a girl who tried to escape from some criminals in an automobile. Then there was a comedy about some cops who kept bumping into each other, then a suspense picture about a couple who find a bag full of banknotes. After that there was a newsreel about the Germans sinking a big passenger ship and then a drama about a young girl who foils a robbery in a boarding house. After that the chase picture came on again.

Every now and then the movie would stop and some words would come up to tell you what was happening or what the characters were saying. Switching from watching pictures to reading was strange at first, but I soon got used to it and forgot I was even doing it.

The time zipped by, and I wanted to stay and watch all the movies again, but I thought Mom and Dad might get mad with me for being out late, so I went home. Turns out they were mad anyway so I might as well have stayed.

GET REAL

Along with comedies, dramas and westerns, nickelodeons showed short summaries of current events called 'newsreels'. One of the biggest stories of 1915 was the sinking of the British passenger ship Lusitania *by a German submarine – 128 Americans were killed, stoking anger against Germany. It was one of the things that led to the USA entering World War I in 1917.*

Wednesday 5ᵗʰ May

Everyone is angry with me for going to the
nickelodeon. Mom and Dad say I should have
brought the nickel home and given it to them
– like it would have made any difference to
us! Mom has straggly black hair and her face
is always scrunched with worry. She worries
about lots of different stuff, but most of all she
worries that we don't have enough money. Dad
works in construction, and he always wears
a dusty blue shirt, black trousers and a grey
cap. He's started worrying about money a lot
too recently.

My sisters Mabel and Betty are mad with me
because I won't stop telling them how much I
loved the movies. As if Mabel ever stops talking
about her job at the telephone exchange, or

Betty ever stops talking about her numbskull boyfriend Ed. Mabel has a large nose and thick eyebrows, which she spends ages plucking in the bathroom when I need to go pee. Betty has piggy eyes and crooked teeth, which she tries to cover with her hand when she's laughing at Ed's lousy jokes.

Thursday 6ᵗʰ May

Mabel got paid today, and gave all her salary to Mom, which meant we could have chicken instead of the usual sardines with our cabbage and potatoes.

Mabel said she'd bought the chicken, so she should get to decide which bits I ate, and I was only allowed the feet.

19

Mom overruled her and I got to eat a leg, but I couldn't enjoy it with Betty and Mabel shooting resentful glances.

I'm sick of my sisters treating me this way. They always tease me by saying I sleep in a closet, which isn't even true. Just because my bedroom is small, and has a metal rail running along the ceiling, doesn't make it a closet. Okay, so maybe the last family to lease this

apartment used it as one, but it's my bedroom now and they're not even allowed in anyway so it's none of their business.

I need to think of some way of getting back at my sisters. Like maybe I could put some cockroaches in an upside-down cup on their bedside table. Then when one of them lifts it, the roaches will run around and they'll be completely terrified.

But they'll know I did it and Mom will punish me. I need to think of something smarter.

Chapter 2
⊢─┤
Making extra money

Friday 7th May

Betty's stupid boyfriend Ed came to dinner tonight. He has neat, centre-parted hair and a thin tie that he pulls right to the top of his shirt. He wears baggy pants high above his waist, and Betty thinks they make him look like Douglas Fairbanks, though I'm reminded more of Charlie Chaplin.

He kept making jokes at my expense, which my sisters would split their sides at. Like he'd say I was a perfect chump, and they'd laugh, then he'd say he took it back because nobody's perfect, and they'd laugh all over again.

I tried to take my mind off his wisecracks by imagining some more ways I could get back at my sisters.

I thought about tying Ed's shoelaces together before he left so he fell downstairs. I'd get revenge on Betty, and teach Ed a lesson about unfunny jokes at the same time.

But then he might actually die and I'll go to jail and maybe meet some people even worse than my sisters in there. Maybe.

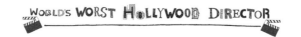

Saturday 8th May

Dad told me to try and get a job in a store today. I've asked before and they all say I'm too young, but he insisted I do it again.

My plan was to ask in some of the clothes shops on Broadway, so I could at least tell him I'd tried. But when I got to the first one I saw a huge crowd and I forgot all about getting a job.

A woman with large, dark eyes and curly brown hair was staggering out. She looked very upset, stopping on the steps to wipe her brow with the back of her hand and swaying from side to side.

The poor woman looked like she was about to faint, and none of the huge crowd were doing anything. Some of them were even grinning. I know L.A. can be a tough city, but I'd never seen anything like that before.

I asked a guy with a bushy moustache what was going on and he said something about a shooting taking place.

This was awful. The woman was the victim of a shooting and no one was helping her. I figured I'd better help if no one else was going to.

I charged through the crowd and grabbed the woman just as she was about to fall. Far from thanking me, she yelled at me for ruining things. Then everyone around her started shouting too, and a tall woman with short black hair lifted a megaphone to her mouth and shouted, 'Cut!'

Uh-oh.

I worked out what was going on and felt my face burning bright red. The tall woman was standing next to a man who was turning the handle of a machine with two metal circles on top of it.

I'd seen a picture of one of those before. It was a movie camera. Far from helping the woman, I'd wrecked her performance. No wonder she was so crabby.

'Get that kid out of here,' shouted the woman with the megaphone.

A woman with short red hair grabbed my arm and pulled me back through the crowd. I tried to explain my mistake, but she just told me to beat it.

GET REAL

Although moviemaking is often criticised for being dominated by men, there were several female directors at work in the early days. They included Alice Guy-Blaché, who pioneered filmmaking in France in the late 19th century before moving to the USA, and Lois Weber, who was the first American woman to direct a feature film. Lois Weber was one of the most important directors in early Hollywood. She started out as a stage actress before writing movie scenarios. She soon began to direct her own scripts, and made hundreds of films in the 1910s and 1920s.

Sunday 9th May

Dad told me to keep looking for a job today, but I went to look for the movie crew again instead. I finally found them on 7th Street. I thought they might recognise me as the girl who'd

ruined things the day before, so I hung at the back of the crowd.

I was just too hooked to stay away. I can't afford to go to the nickelodeon, so watching them make movies is the only way I can get to see them at all.

They were filming a scene where the actress with the curly hair confronts a man in a brown hat.

The actress would wait at the top of the street, then the woman with the megaphone would shout 'Action' and a man would turn the handle on the camera.

The actress and the actor would play their scene and the woman would yell into the megaphone about how they were meant to be

feeling. You're angry, now you're torn, now
you're upset, that kind of stuff. Then she'd yell
'Cut!' and tell them to do it again.

It didn't look like much from the back of the
crowd, but I expected it would be more dramatic
when projected onto a wall with someone
playing the piano along with it.

Cut!

The woman with the megaphone went over to the woman with red hair and pointed at me. I thought she might have recognised me as the one who'd ruined everything, so I got ready to run away.

The woman with red hair stepped over. But instead of getting angry, she said we needed extras for the scene, and asked if anyone wanted to do it.

I had no idea what an extra was, but if it had something to do with helping out on the movie, I wanted to do it.

I shot my hand up and pushed to the front. The woman with red hair grabbed my arm and yanked me forward. Then she pulled out another five people from the crowd and pointed to a spot on the pavement where we would have to wait.

It turned out that being an extra meant I would appear in the movie, although only as part of a crowd. The woman with the megaphone apparently thought it would be more exciting if the actress had to push her way down a very busy street.

The woman shouted 'Action' and we made our way along the sidewalk while the actress shoved past. We did it a couple more times and then we were done.

The other extras left, but I hung around with the crew and nobody stopped me. Most of them were too busy to talk, but I managed to speak to the woman with the red hair, who's called Alma. She works as an assistant to the woman with the megaphone, who's called Dolores, and is directing the picture.

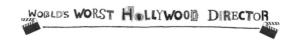

Dolores always wants everything to be perfect, which is why she keeps getting everyone to do it over and over again. Alma is kind of annoyed about this, but I said it was good that Dolores wanted the movie to be amazing and if I were a director I'd do just the same.

She said the cameraman was called Wallace and the actors were called Loretta Cooke and Wade Arnold. I nodded like I'd heard of them.

They're filming around East Second Street Tuesday through Thursday, and I'm going to keep coming back and watching them until they tell me to stop.

GET REAL

*In 1915, movies were shot on hand-cranked
cameras like the popular Bell and Howell
model, which had two large reels on top.
The roll of film started out in the front one,
and it would go down past the lens and
back up into the rear one as the handle
was turned. These kinds of cameras took
hundreds of still images that gave the
illusion of movement when played back.*

Monday 10ᵗʰ May

My family weren't impressed when I told them
I'd been an extra. Dad got angry that I'd been
watching movie people instead of looking for a
job. And Betty and Mabel said I was pathetic
for getting so excited about being in a moving
picture for one second like I was a real actress
all of a sudden.

To shut them up, I pretended Dolores had been
so impressed by my performance she'd asked
me to come back for more scenes. I invented
a name and personality for my character. I
said she was called Constance and she was so
generous and kind to others that she often went
without food and drink herself.

They kept glancing at each other and rolling
their eyes like always, but I could tell it was
making them mad. Neither of them has ever
done anything as impressive as starring in a
moving picture.

When I went to my room I found my sisters had
hung their dresses on the rail. They keep doing
this and pretending they've forgotten it's my
room and not a closet.

I threw their dresses out into the hallway,
which of course meant they spent the evening

yelling at me for creasing their clothes. I'll snip
them into rags next time they do it.

Tuesday 11th May

I got up early and went to East Second Street,
but no one was there. I thought Alma might
have been lying but then I saw her pull up in
an automobile. Dolores and Wallace got out of
the back and set up the camera in front of a
metal stairwell leading up to some apartments.

I hadn't been given the wrong address after
all. I'd just been so keen I'd turned up before
everyone else.

I asked Dolores if I could be an extra, and she
said she'd call me over if she thought the scene
needed it.

38

Loretta Cooke soon arrived in another automobile. Alma arranged Loretta's hat and hair as they waited to film the scene.

Dolores talked her through the action from behind the camera. She said Loretta had to run along the street looking distressed, then make her way up to the apartment. I wondered if Loretta got tired having to be so upset all the time.

She kept having to do the scene over and I could tell Dolores wasn't happy, so I asked if she wanted to try using an extra. She stared at me for a moment, then said it might put more drama into the scene if I came the opposite way carrying a bag of groceries and bumped into Loretta.

Alma rushed off to buy a paper bag full of fruit and vegetables. I decided my character of Constance was probably taking them to the poor and needy, though I wasn't sure how to put this across in my performance. I wondered if Dolores could put up some sort of title about it.

Dolores gave me the groceries and called 'Action!' The first time I was too slow, and Loretta reached the stairs before I got to her.

We went again, and I made sure to go faster. Unfortunately, I went so much quicker that I slammed right into Loretta and fell to the ground, spilling my vegetables everywhere. I tried to scramble up, but I slipped on a cabbage and accidentally dragged Loretta down too. Dolores yelled that she was trying to put more drama in the scene, not more comedy.

We took a moment for Loretta to brush the squashed tomatoes from her dress, and then tried again.

The next time started out perfectly. I bumped
into Loretta, and she pushed past me. But
then I thought it wouldn't fit with Constance's

character to bump into someone and let them go without checking they were okay, so I turned and ran after her.

Dolores yelled 'Cut!' and asked what I was doing. I explained all about the character I'd created and her generous nature. She said I was just an extra and the audience wouldn't care if I was off to help someone or boil a puppy.

We did it again, and this time I got it all right. I strode along the sidewalk, bumped into Loretta, and continued along, even though this isn't what Constance would actually do.

Dolores said everyone could move on, which I think was her way of saying I'd done well. I went over and thanked her for letting me be an extra again.

She asked what I meant by 'again'. I told her I'd been in the crowd scene on Thursday, and she got really mad. She said that this scene followed right on from that one, and Loretta could hardly walk past the same girl twice. She said I'd wasted everyone's time and we couldn't use the scene.

It was really mean of her to shout at me in front of everyone like that. She could at least have taken the megaphone away from her mouth first.

Wednesday 12th May

I can't believe my performance as Constance will never be seen. Maybe audiences would have loved her so much she'd have been given her own movie. Now I'll never know.

I got no sympathy at home, of course. Dad kept going on about money and Mom said actors and movie-makers were bad people and I should stay away from them.

Betty said I was stupid for wanting to be in moving pictures in the first place, because they're just cheap versions of plays, and people with class go to see them instead.

She's never been to one herself, of course, and Dad would never let her. He got mad with me for spending a nickel going to movies, so he's hardly going to let her spend a dollar on a show.

I've never been to a play either, but I don't see why everyone thinks they are so much better than movies. Sure, you hear the actors speak, but there's a lot of good stuff you can only do in the movies.

The camera can go right up to the actor's face so you can see their expressions. Only the people at the front get that with plays. And you can show real places instead of just sets. You can jump between different scenes much quicker too.

The movies are still pretty new. I bet no one thought plays were so fancy either when they first came along.

Chapter 3

Big ideas

Thursday 13th May

I couldn't stop myself going back to watch
Dolores and her crew today, even though I
knew I wouldn't be welcome after yesterday.

I tried to keep to the back of the crowd, but
most of the other onlookers got bored and
walked away, so I kept finding myself at the
front again.

They were filming the end of the movie, where
Loretta and Wade make up and embrace.

Between takes Dolores kept talking to a guy
in a brown suit with thick-rimmed glasses and
hair that stuck straight up. At first I thought
they were discussing someone they knew
who had been attacked by robbers, but I soon
worked out they were coming up with an idea
for a new movie.

The man in the glasses kept suggesting ideas to Dolores, but she didn't like any of them.

I remembered the robbery story I'd come up with outside the nickelodeon, and wondered if Dolores would like to hear it.

When she'd finished shooting the scene again, I tapped her on the shoulder. I told her my idea about the telephone girl racing to the house of the rich lady to save her from the robbers.

Dolores stared at me with her nostrils flaring. She looked like she was going to yell again, so I flinched back.

I was right. She did start shouting. But not at me.

She turned to the man wearing the pair of thick-rimmed glasses and screamed about how

Mr. Cheeseman was wasting money on him when a kid from the street could come up with better ideas.

The man with the glasses threw his notepad and pencil to the floor and told Dolores to film my story instead if it was so good.

Dolores picked up the pencil and pad and handed them to me. She told me to write down my scenario, which I guessed was her word for story.

I sat on the sidewalk and tried to get it all down. I must have used up half the guy's pad because I kept ripping pages out and screwing them up.

I needed to add new bits to the race against time section, just to make sure it was action-packed. I wrote a scene where the telephone girl gets her bicycle stuck in the tracks just as a train is speeding towards her. She abandons her bicycle, jumps on the train, then leaps off that too just before it explodes on a collapsing bridge and crashes into a river.

I thought about how angry Dad would be if I didn't ask for money, so I flipped the paper over, wrote my name and address and added that they had to give me a dollar if they used my story and if they didn't I'd tell the police.

I didn't really think the cops would care. But I thought it might scare them into paying. After all, a dollar can't be much to these movie people, but we could use an extra one right about now.

When I was finally done, I handed my sheet of paper to Dolores and asked if she'd make it into a movie. She said it was pretty good, but she'd have to run it past Rex Cheeseman, the guy she works for.

Apparently, he's a big producer who's just moved his studio from New Jersey to a ranch in the mountains north of here. He's snapped up all the best directors, including Dolores, and has to approve all the scenarios before they can be made.

There's nothing I can do now except hope Mr Cheeseman likes my script.

GET REAL

Many American movie companies relocated from the East Coast to Hollywood in the 1910s. One of the biggest was Universal Pictures, owned by a German immigrant named Carl Laemmle. In 1915, he opened Universal City on the site of a farm in the San Fernando Valley. The company is still based there today, and the location is also home to the incredibly popular Universal Studios theme park.

Carl Laemmle opened his first nickelodeon in 1906, and moved into producing movies, eventually becoming one of the most powerful figures in early Hollywood.

Friday 14th May

I keep checking our letter box for my dollar,
but all I can find is love letters from Ed. Betty
always reads them out like I'm going to be
jealous, but they just make me feel sick. He
keeps saying he's going to buy an automobile
and drive Betty down to the beach so they
can watch the sunset and he can declare his
undying love 'somewhere real swell'. He's been
promising this for weeks, but there's no sign of
any automobile yet.

Maybe I should write a fake break-up note from him and put it in our letter box. I could come up with a dramatic story about how he was kidnapped by bandits and taken to Mexico or something. But then imagine how crazy everyone would be when they found out it was a lie.

There must be a better way to get back at my sisters. It would have to be something that makes them both mad, but that Mom and Dad can't blame me for.

Saturday 15ᵗʰ May

Today I made the mistake of telling my sisters about my movie idea. They just looked at each other and giggled like it was the stupidest thing ever, even though they've never been to the movies and wouldn't know what makes a good one anyway.

I'm glad I handed my movie idea straight to Dolores. If I'd taken it home to run past my sisters, they'd have put me off ever showing it to anyone.

They're always like this. They say everything was better for them before I came along, because they could afford more stuff and didn't have to share a room. Though Mabel was only five and Betty was six when I was born, so I bet they don't remember that much really.

And at least having me to pick on keeps them close. They're always laughing together and reading each other bits from magazines. I bet if I weren't here they'd be picking on each other all the time.

Anyway, it doesn't matter what my sisters think. It's Mr Cheeseman's verdict that counts. I'll just have to hope he delivers it soon.

Sunday 16th May

Mabel came running upstairs with a letter this morning and she pretended it was addressed to me to make me think Dolores had replied. But just as she was about to hand it over she announced that she'd read the name wrong and really it was just another love letter for Betty.

What a terrible start to the day. Not only did I have my hopes dashed, but I had to listen to Ed's awful words about how Betty was 'a real knockout' and he was close to buying his automobile so they could have some 'neat adventures' together.

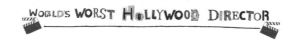

Monday 17ᵗʰ May

We were all sitting at the table this morning eating our breakfast grape-nuts when we heard the 'ahooga ahooga' of an automobile horn on the street outside our apartment.

Betty clasped her hands to her chest and declared it was Ed. We all rushed to the window, and even I was expecting to see the grinning sap behind the wheel.

But it wasn't him at all. Dolores and Alma were sitting in the automobile. And they were waving at me.

I scrambled down the stairs, and the others followed. Alma was at the steering wheel and Dolores was behind her, sitting on a long seat that looked like a couch.

Dolores said she liked my scenario and wanted me to come to Cheeseman City to work on some ideas with her. Dad interrupted right away to ask how much money I'd get. Dolores said it wasn't up to her, but she'd do her best.

Mom questioned Dolores about where exactly I was going and what time I'd be back. I couldn't believe she was letting her worrying get in the way of the sort of incredible opportunity that almost never happens.

But Dad came to the rescue for once. He shrugged and said I could go, as long as there would be some money at some point.

I climbed in next to Dolores and grinned at Betty and Mabel. I could see them scowling and muttering as we drove away, and I felt like it had already been worth it whether I got my dollar or not.

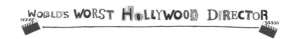

Alma sped away down the street, honking at pedestrians and yelling at them to get out of the way rather than slowing down.

Riding in the automobile was fun, but I didn't get much time to enjoy it. Dolores shoved a notepad into my hand and ran off a list of things she wanted to change about my scenario.

Every time I suggested something, Dolores would say it was good, then stare into the distance and say it wouldn't work.

I tried to write down everything she was saying, but the automobile bumped up and down so much that the notepad ended up looking more like a young child's drawing than a movie scenario.

Soon we were leaving the last houses of Los Angeles behind and heading out into the mountains. There were no other automobiles around, but Alma kept glancing about anyway. I asked if she was checking for bandits, but she said she was more worried about patents men.

I had no idea who these patents men were, but I hoped we didn't meet them if they were scarier than bandits.

We soon approached a wide archway that linked two square white buildings. A banner stretching across it read, 'Welcome to Cheeseman City – Capital of the Movie

World'. On one of the white buildings there was a poster of a tall grinning man with white hair. The words, 'Rex Cheeseman, King of the Movies' were painted above him.

A man in a long coat who must have been very hot opened a gate and we drove in. Rex Cheeseman might have been overdoing it when he called his movie-making ranch a 'city'. Beyond the grand entrance were just two rows of low white buildings that led to a huge barn. There was a long outdoor stage at the far end of the ranch, split into different sets where cowboys, gangsters and smart city folk performed for people with megaphones.

It was a very impressive ranch, and Mr Cheeseman must really be someone who believes movies are more than just a fad, but it was hardly a city. I suppose if you're in the business of making up stories, you need to make them up about yourself too. Maybe I should change my name to Jewel or Petal or Strawberry Ice Cream or something.

We pulled up outside one of the white buildings and went in. Inside were three narrow desks with typewriters on. The floor was covered in so many screwed up bits of paper it looked like a department store Christmas scene.

The man with thick-rimmed glasses, who turned out to be called Mortimer, was sitting behind the desk on the right and tapping on a typewriter. Dolores pulled his sheet out, glanced at it, said it didn't work and tossed it over her shoulder.

Mortimer inserted a new sheet and continued tapping. The room was very stuffy, and sweat was pouring down his face as he hammered at

the keys. It looked like making up stories was just as exhausting as the construction work Dad does.

A small man with white hair and a spotless white suit walked in. It was nice to see someone my height around the place, as most movie folk seemed to be giants. I could tell right away that he was important, because two guys wearing sun visor hats chased after him, jabbering and waving bits of paper. It was only when one of them called him Mr Cheeseman that I realised this was the guy himself.

Mr Cheeseman raised a hand and the men shut up right away. He pointed at me and asked if I was the little lady called Clara who'd written the scenario about the telephone exchange girl. He had a thick German accent, and I wondered if he'd changed his name to make it sound more American.

I said I was, and he rubbed his chin and gazed at me. He asked what my dad does, and I told him he works in construction. He said it was a tough business, with lots of people getting laid off right now, but it was real work, and I was just the kind of real person the studio needed. He then turned to Mortimer and yelled at him for being a privileged Ivy League layabout who knew nothing of the world.

I asked if this meant he was going to make my movie, and he said no, because the chase scene was too expensive. Darn it! I knew I shouldn't have overdone it with that exploding train.

But he said the scenario was a good calling card, and that Dolores should take me on as an assistant.

He said I could help Dolores think of the sort of stories that would appeal to regular viewers, instead of creeps from Harvard University who'd never had it tough. He looked at Mortimer again when he said this. I wondered why he kept Mortimer around if he hated him so much.

Mr Cheeseman launched into a story about how poor he'd been as a child. At first I thought he was telling me a movie idea and I should write it down, but then I realised he was actually making some sort of point about ordinary people like me.

Mr Cheeseman made it sound good to be ordinary, and I guess it is. But if he'd left a gap for me to talk, I'd have told him I'm not all that ordinary really. I can wiggle my ears and lick my elbow, for example.

The men on either side of Mr Cheeseman started yapping and flapping again and he turned to leave. It had all happened so fast I was a little confused. He'd assumed I'd want to come and work with Dolores, which I did. But he'd also managed to talk about everything except whether I'd get paid. For Dad's sake, I needed to at least raise this.

I tugged on the sleeve of Mr Cheeseman's suit and said I'd still like my dollar even though they weren't making my movie. He took a silk handkerchief out of his pocket and mopped the sweat from his forehead. Then he said I'd driven a hard bargain and could have a dollar per week.

I'd only been looking for a dollar for the story he didn't use, but getting one every week sounded pretty good, so I kept my mouth shut.

As Alma drove me home, I thought of all the brilliant stuff I could do with my weekly dollar. I could go to Milton's Diner, which is two blocks away from our apartment, and order waffles, ice cream, doughnuts, cinnamon toast and lemonade all at once. Or I could save up to buy fancy clothes from the shops on Broadway. Or I could buy five candy bars every day and eat them in front of Betty and Mabel without sharing a single piece.

GET REAL

The Motion Pictures Patents Company was formed in 1908 by a group of powerful business owners including Thomas Edison, and it aimed to limit how movies were made. They believed they had the exclusive right to use movie cameras, and hired violent thugs to break up productions they hadn't licensed. They were based on the East Coast of the USA, and many filmmakers moved to Hollywood to get away from them.

So the world's most famous inventor Thomas Edison also helped to invent Hollywood, even if he didn't mean to.

Chapter 4

Making movies

Tuesday 18th May

So much for buying five candy bars a day. When I told Dad about my weekly dollar, he insisted I hand it over to him every time. He even got mad at me for not asking for more. So that's the thanks I get?

Why is he so obsessed with money anyway? We seem to do okay between what he makes and what Mabel makes. It's not like we can't eat or that our landlord is trying to throw us out onto the streets.

75

Not that I'll have much time to spend money anyway, I suppose. Alma arrived at our apartment at seven this morning, and I climbed in next to Dolores again. She said they'd be round at the same time every day, and she hasn't mentioned anything about days off. Her whole life is based around work, and she doesn't seem to have a husband or children or even a dog.

I spent the whole morning scribbling ideas down and then crossing them out in that small, sweaty office. I'm so used to screwing up bits of paper and throwing them across the room that I nearly did it with this journal page.

Dolores went out for a meeting with Mr Cheeseman at noon, and I thought that might be a chance for a break, but she told Mortimer and I to write three new scenarios before she got back.

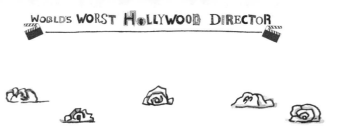

When Dolores had gone, I asked Mortimer why she never liked his ideas. He said she did at first, but then she decided he was out of touch with regular moviegoers, even though he thinks a good story is a good story whether it's written by someone who lives in a castle or a slum.

I kind of agree. Dolores and Mr Cheeseman think I'll have some magic touch because I come from a more ordinary household than Mortimer, but it's not like I spend all my time being chased by robbers or battling bandits or doing any of the other stuff people in moving pictures do.

I worked even harder in the afternoon, and I was so exhausted on the ride home that I could hardly keep awake. But then we drove past an employment agency with a huge crowd of desperate men at the door, and I was glad someone wanted me to work for them, even if it was tough.

One of the men looked so much like Dad that I had to stop myself waving to him. Shows how tired I was.

Wednesday 19th May

Dolores took me into the laboratory today. This is where all the film from the cameras is placed onto wooden racks and dipped into a very smelly liquid.

Afterwards, they hang it up to dry and take it to another room where it can be chopped and glued into the right sequence, which is called 'editing'. Finally, they take it into a room with a projector and watch it back, then they show it to Mr Cheeseman, who decides if it's ready to send out to theatres or not.

You must never show him your movie just before lunch. He gets in a bad mood when he's hungry and wants to change everything. Dolores once showed him the cut of a crime picture while his stomach was rumbling and he insisted she shoot a new ending where all the cops and criminals perform a dance routine up and down some steps. He said it would make the picture more upbeat, but it just made it confusing and no theatres would take it.

Today Dolores was editing *For Her Son*, the movie I saw her shooting with Loretta and

Wade. As well as getting the scenes in the right order, she wanted to make sure they were all the right length, which is called 'pacing'. She kept getting one of the lab guys called Carlyle to chop the film up and glue bits of it together. Then she'd run it through her fingers in front of a light to get an idea of what it would look like when projected.

Dolores cut out the crowd scene where I was an extra, which was kind of annoying. But then she included the scene where I bumped into Loretta instead, so I got a bigger role. Maybe Constance will be a smash with audiences after all.

After six hours of messing with the film, Dolores declared she was ready to view it through the projector. When it was done, she said it was all wrong and she wanted to start over and edit all the footage again.

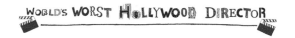

Carlyle said he'd have to ask Mr Cheeseman
for extra funds, and Dolores stormed out. After
she left, Carlyle said this happens every time.
Mr Cheeseman never agrees to the additional
budget, and Dolores moves on to her next movie.

GET REAL

One of the things that helped cinema develop from a cheap novelty to an exciting new form of storytelling was editing. Filmmakers found clever ways of cutting between different scenes, and between different camera angles within scenes. Editing is done digitally now, but in the early days it was done by chopping up strips of film and gluing them together.

Thursday 20th May

Just like Carlyle said, Mr Cheeseman won't let Dolores recut her movie. He watched it right after lunch and said it was fine to send out.

Dolores didn't fight back, and was pretty distracted anyway by a huge argument she was having with Mortimer about the new fashion for feature-length movies. Mortimer has seen *The Birth of a Nation*, which runs for a crazily long three hours. He says it was as absorbing as watching a play or reading a book and he thinks all movies will be feature-length soon.

Dolores says audiences will still prefer to see one-reel pictures once all the talk about *The Birth of a Nation* has died down. After all, why would they settle for one type of story when they can see four or five?

It's weird that she doesn't even want to go and see *The Birth of a Nation* to make her mind up properly. She says she can't afford to take three hours out of her day, though I'm sure it would be worthwhile if Mortimer is to be believed.

I guess Mortimer does have some weird predictions about the movies, though. He thinks that one day they'll line up sound recordings with movies so audiences can hear the actors talk. As if anyone would want that.

GET REAL

Early movies typically lasted between 10 and 16 minutes, the length of one reel of 35-millimetre film. Some directors wanted to make longer films, but it wasn't easy. Most people assumed audiences wouldn't want them, and the Motion Picture Patents Company tried to restrict movie length.

An Australian feature-length movie called
The Story of the Kelly Gang *was made in*
1906. But the one that showed studios how
much money long films could make was
D.W. Griffith's The Birth of a Nation *in*
1915. While it was a major leap forward
for movie-making, it was condemned for
being racist, and helped to rekindle the
Ku Klux Klan, an organisation that hated
black people.

Friday 21st May

Today I helped Carlyle carry some heavy film
containers from the laboratory to the main gate.

Lugging the reels around in the heat made me
feel dizzy, and I should have stopped to get a
drink, but I wanted to get it over with so I could
go back and help Dolores and Mortimer come
up with new ideas.

85

I was almost done when I noticed two suspicious figures hanging around one of the offices. I put the film cans down and watched them closely.

A tall man and a short man were walking around the side of the white building. They were scowling and glancing around, like they were up to no good. They had dusty black suits, scuffed shoes and dirty white shirts.

I called over at them, but they ignored me.

The men reached the door and the tall one tried the handle. It was locked, but the short one took a long pin out of his pocket and shoved it into the lock.

So that's what they were up to. Breaking into our offices to steal our equipment. And there was no one around to stop them but me. I was going to have to be brave.

I ran over to the thugs and told them to stop.

They didn't respond, so I gave them both firm slaps. The little one asked what I was doing. He didn't sound much like a street hood. He sounded kind of rich, like a lawyer or a bank clerk or... an actor. Uh-oh.

I heard a man shouting 'cut' and I realised what I'd done. I apologised and backed off, but the director came running over and yelled at me for ruining his shot. He was a short, bald man wearing baggy pants and grasping a megaphone.

He'd been filming the actors from a distance in a wide shot, and I'd totally missed him.

I apologised and backed off, hoping he'd go away. But he kept following and shouting. His face went red and the wispy hairs at the side of his head shook back and forth as he worked himself into a rage.

All along the row of offices, people stepped out to look. I turned and raced for our office, hoping I could get in before Dolores saw.

No luck. She was standing in the doorway and wincing at all the chaos I was causing.

Saturday 22nd May

There was no mention of my little mistake when Alma and Dolores came to pick me up this morning. Dolores was so excited about her new movie she seemed to have forgotten it.

Mr Cheeseman has approved a scenario she
wrote with Mortimer called *The Bank Robbery*,
and I had to spend today running around
and passing instructions from Dolores to
prop builders, carpenters and the wardrobe
department.

We're shooting this movie on the studio stage, so sets will have to be built for each scene. Even the indoor scenes have to be shot outdoors so there's enough light to make the picture clear. This means we could get unlucky and have to stop for bad weather. I'm sure viewers would notice if a storm suddenly hit in the middle of a bank.

I had to keep scribbling down all the measurements for the bank set on scraps of notepaper and take them over to the carpenters, who work in a big yard at the back of the laboratory.

They were a little confused at times, probably because Dolores kept changing her mind so much. In the end, I had to tell them to build what it said on the paper and stop questioning absolutely everything.

I really need a day off tomorrow after all that running around, but that doesn't happen in the world of Dolores, even on a Sunday. But I'm getting the next best thing. We're going to a nickelodeon on Broadway to watch *For Her Son*.

Dolores says she wants to know how it's playing in theatres. I'm not sure what that means or how it would be different from watching it in the studio projection room, but if I get to watch movies all day, it's fine with me.

GET REAL

While electric lights powerful enough for indoor filming existed in 1915, the cheapest and best source of light was still the sun. Universal City featured an outdoor stage that was 90 metres long and divided into segments so several different films could be shot at once. A 'DON'T SHOOT' sign would be raised if the weather became too cloudy.

Sunday 23rd May

Okay, so that wasn't quite the relaxing day I
was hoping for. I met Dolores and Alma outside
the nickelodeon at noon, and they handed our
coins over.

There was a melodrama showing called *Broken
Heart at the Altar*, which was about a plain girl
whose fiancé abandons her on their wedding
day. After a big chase, the girl's family catch
the absent groom and talk him round. But the
twist is that she doesn't want to marry him
after all because she can finally see what a heel
he is. So the broken heart mentioned in the title
is his, not hers.

I thought it was pretty good, but Dolores ruined
it by yakking all the way through, explaining
how the director should have filmed each scene,
and why the casting was all wrong.

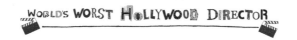

Dolores enjoyed the next film more, which was a comedy about a restaurant owner who gets mixed up with crooks. The whole thing ended up in a nutty chase in which a fruit vendor kept getting his cart knocked over as soon as he'd loaded all the apples and oranges back on.

Dolores insisted on explaining why all the jokes worked and how good the editing was. She's been involved in making pictures for so long that this is what she does instead of laughing now. I wonder if she'd do the same if she saw someone slip on a banana skin in real life.

Finally, it was time for our movie, *For Her Son*. Dolores leant forward and nodded through the opening scenes in which Loretta starts to worry that her husband is actually a criminal. But she soon started to mutter to herself and I could tell she wasn't happy.

I wondered if she was upset with the pianist, a woman wearing thick spectacles who kept playing wrong notes and stopping to flip the pages of her sheet music. But it's not like you'd expect the musicians in a local nickelodeon to be brilliant. Especially the ones working the Sunday lunchtime shift.

94

I got lost in the story until the bit where I appeared on the screen, which snapped me out of it. Seeing a huge version of myself on the wall was really strange, like looking into a gigantic fairground mirror. It must be even weirder if you're the star and you have to watch yourself all the way through.

Dolores was still shuffling around and muttering, so I asked her what was wrong. She said they were running the film far too fast. Now that she mentioned it, Loretta did seem to be running around at a crazy pace.

Dolores grabbed my arm and yanked me up. I thought she was going to leave, but she pulled me over to the back of the theatre. She raced up a ladder and we followed her into a small, stuffy room with big sheets of metal nailed to the walls.

A man wearing a white shirt that was drenched with sweat was standing next to a large machine with spinning rolls of film.

He asked Dolores what she wanted, and she said he was showing her movie wrong. She shoved him out of the way and fiddled with a switch on the side of his machine. Then she peered out of the hole in the front of his booth and said it was better.

The sweaty man told her to get out and let him do his job. He said he'd started the programme late and needed to make the time up somewhere. He then made things worse for himself by saying her movie could do with a little extra zip anyway.

Alma and I had to pretty much drag Dolores out of the movie theatre after that. She wants to

report the man to the company that distributes our movies, but she needs to let it go. We can't go around every movie theatre in the world telling them how to play our movie.

GET REAL

The speed at which movies were projected wasn't set at a standard level until the sound era in the late 1920s, when the picture had to match up with dialogue. In the silent era, theatres would often speed up films to make them fit into particular time slots.

Monday 24th May

Today was even worse than usual. After a morning of gathering props for the robbery movie, Alma announced that the carpenters had finished the bank set, and called us over.

My heart sank as I approached the stage. The set was nothing like the one Dolores had asked for, and I just knew I'd get the blame somehow.

There was a wide wooden counter with windows and overhanging lamps. It was just as Dolores had sketched, with one important difference. It was far too small.

Dolores asked the carpenter what was going on, and he pulled out the scrap of paper with the instructions on it that I'd given him.

I looked at it and winced. In all my confusion about the ever-changing instructions, I'd

written the total height of the set as five feet instead of eight. No wonder the carpenters had been so confused.

I felt myself blushing bright red as Dolores and the carpenter argued. Two actors and an actress approached the set, and I heard one of the carpenters explaining that the little girl had messed things up.

The actors playing the gangsters and the actress playing the bank teller tried to take their positions, but first of all they had to crouch to see each other through the bank counter window.

Dolores said she wouldn't shoot until the carpenters fixed the set, and they said it would need totally rebuilding, and that they didn't have the time.

Eventually, Mr Cheeseman was called out of his office. He was holding a spoon, wearing a bib covered in soup stains, and scowling.

Dolores explained the situation and he told her to lose the bank scene and explain it with a title card. Dolores said that when someone goes to see a movie called *The Bank Robbery*, they might at least expect to see a bank getting robbed at some point. Mr Cheeseman suggested calling it *After the Bank Robbery*, and I could see Dolores taking deep breaths to try to calm herself down.

Mr Cheeseman made a series of suggestions, each of which pushed Dolores closer to the edge.

He said all the characters could be giants and we could build the other sets to the same scale and call it *Bank Robbery in Giantsville*. He then suggested we could use child performers instead and paint moustaches on them so they looked older. And he even suggested including a new opening scene in which all three characters lose their legs in a gas explosion.

In the end, one of the carpenters suggested making the actors kneel on the small carts they use for moving bits of wood around, and filming them from the waist up.

Dolores wasn't happy, but she had no choice. She either had to agree or lose the picture altogether.

Wallace set his camera at a lower level, and the confused actors took their places on the tiny carts so they could be wheeled in and out of shot.

I think the scene will look kind of okay, though the movement of the actors will be a little strange. Dolores is really mad with me, though. I don't think she's even speaking to me.

GET REAL

Large teams of carpenters were employed by movie studios. At first their job was just to create realistic backdrops. But movies such as The Cabinet of Doctor Caligari *in 1920 showed that strange and distorted sets could be used to great effect. The design of a movie could be just as important as its casting and photography. 'Art directors' were hired to take charge of the overall look of movies.*

Tuesday 25th May

We were done with the miniature bank set today, thankfully. We moved onto a location shoot on 8th Street. It was near enough for me to walk, which was lucky. Sitting next to Dolores in the automobile while she's so mad with me would have been awkward.

When I got there I asked Dolores what she wanted me to do, and she told me to go and help Alma.

I wondered how long it would be before she started asking me to stay away from the shoots altogether. I skulked over to Alma and asked if she thought Dolores might get rid of me because of all my mistakes.

She told me not to worry about it. She said Dolores had fired and then rehired Mortimer over ten times. She always takes him back right away.

I tried my best to help Alma so Dolores could see I was being useful. The actors playing the gangsters were filming a chase scene, and their hats kept blowing off, so I picked them up and gave them back every time.

Dolores made them do the scene over and over again, even though they were getting tired. Finally, she said they'd done it, and the actors collapsed on the pavement. She announced they could take twenty minutes for lunch before moving onto the next chase scene, and they groaned.

I heard one of them grumbling about how he never had to put up with this in plays. I felt kind of sorry for him, but I also doubted he'd be playing a criminal in a chase picture if Broadway wanted him.

GET REAL

At first, stage actors looked down on movie actors, who they thought were wasting their talents on a silly fad. But things gradually changed. The French actress Sarah Bernhardt, reckoned to be the best in the world, reproduced some of her famous stage roles in a series of popular movies. Soon screen actors like Mary Pickford and Douglas Fairbanks became incredibly rich, famous and powerful, and other actors decided movies might not be so silly after all.

Wednesday 26ᵗʰ May

We were meant to have moved to an alleyway off Main Street today, but when I got there I saw a note stuck to a lamppost telling us to go back to 8th Street, where we filmed yesterday.

I figured something must have gone wrong with the footage so we had to do it again, but I was sure it couldn't be my fault this time.

When I got back to 8th I asked Alma what the problem was. She winced and explained that I'd given the actors the wrong hats. One had been wearing a light brown hat and the other a black hat. I'd switched them round by mistake, and now the scenes we shot yesterday don't match the earlier footage.

I doubted many viewers would notice, but it's the sort of thing that matters to Dolores, so she wanted to redo everything.

I couldn't believe I'd only done one thing yesterday, and I'd still managed to spoil the whole shoot.

At least Dolores was happy to move on after just three takes this time. But there was another problem when we got to the alleyway.

Dolores had chosen a young actress called Blanche to play the role of a girl who confronts the gangsters. But there was no sign of her near Main Street, so she must have got confused by the location switch.

Dolores sent Alma off to find Blanche, and in the meantime paced up and down and muttered about how far behind schedule we were getting.

Finally, I had a chance to make things up to her. Blanche was twenty years old, but she was playing a much younger character. It was a role I could step into if we were desperate.

I suggested to Dolores that I play Blanche's role. She shrugged, glanced around the street again, and finally said that I might as well give it a try.

I jumped into the costume, which was a white dress with a red shawl. It fitted pretty well, which I took as a good sign.

Dolores took me through what she wanted from my performance. I had to show I was conflicted between my fear of the gangsters and my determination to get justice for my father, who they had just robbed.

It sounded like a tough bit of acting for my first real try. But I could be a natural for all I knew.

We went right into a take. I wondered what someone would look like if they were torn between two strong emotions. I tried rubbing my chin and staring into the sky like I was making a big decision.

Dolores sighed and told me to try again. This time I attempted to put across the character's fear by biting my fingernails and looking from side to side.

Dolores said it still wasn't right. We went again, and I tried to show the character's determination by grinning and punching the air.

Umm... does this work?

She still didn't like it. I couldn't think of a gesture that would put across conflict, fear and determination all at once. In the end, I settled on swooning with the back of my hand pressed against my forehead. This is something I'd seen Loretta do a lot in *For Her Son*, so I thought it might be a good general way of putting across the emotion.

Finally, Dolores said I'd done well and we could move on to the scene where I confront the gangsters. But just as she said it, Alma arrived with Blanche.

This meant she could shoot the scene as we'd planned and my acting skills wouldn't be needed. I was secretly quite relieved. I don't think I'd have got away with swooning in every scene, and that was the only bit of acting I could really do.

Chapter 5

Plot twists

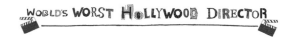
Thursday 27th May

I have much more respect for actors after my little try yesterday. I used to think they were just vain and whiny, which is true, but what they do is really hard. Expressing different emotions while someone yells at you through a megaphone is tough. Especially when you have a crowd staring at you.

I suppose they get to see their faces projected onto walls as a reward, if that's the sort of thing they like. And the popular ones get fans interrupting them while they're trying to eat or walk down the street, although that sounds more like a punishment.

Forget acting. I want to be on the other side of the camera. Coming up with great stories and bringing them to life is what I should be doing.

If I'm going to make things up with Dolores, I need to go back to the thing that made her hire me in the first place. I need to come up with another great scenario, and this time it will have to be cheap enough for Mr Cheeseman to agree to it.

I went straight to my room when I got home so I could work on some new ideas. I found that my sisters had hung one of Dad's workshirts on the rail when I got there, but I ignored it rather than giving them the fight they wanted.

Dad's shirts don't seem to get as dusty as they used to, anyway. He was working out on the aqueduct until recently, and he used to come home covered in dirt, but I think he must have moved on to a different site.

I've come up with three ideas now. I just have to hope they're good enough to turn things around with Dolores.

Friday 28th May

I got to the location early this morning, and as soon as Dolores arrived, I took her through all my ideas.

One was about a hypnotist who uses his powers to steal money from rich old ladies. Another was about a poor street singer who falls for a rich girl. And another was about a couple who have their jewels stolen by a gang of thieves.

Dolores said they all sounded good and I should go home and write them as full scenarios.

At first I was pleased she liked my ideas, but then I thought it might just be a way of telling me to go away.

I told her I could stay on the shoot and write them, so she could still get my help if she needed it.

I perched on the edge of the pavement and worked on my ideas. Turns out my help wasn't wanted. That's okay. I know I've made some mistakes. But Dolores will forgive them all when she reads my great stories.

Saturday 29th May

I showed my scenarios to Dolores today and she said the one about the stolen jewels had real promise but needed a good twist. She asked if I wanted to go away and work on it for a couple of days, and I got worried again that she might be trying to get rid of me.

But then she took a few minutes away from preparing her shoot to take me through the ways she tries to surprise audiences when she's writing scenarios, so I figured it wasn't just her sneaky way of firing me.

Plus she gave me two dollars of her own money so I could work in a diner if I wanted. She said going somewhere different to work can be helpful when you're coming up with ideas.

She's going to call round in the automobile with Alma on Wednesday, and she wants me to have a brilliant scenario finished by then.

I snatched the money out of Dolores's hand and promised I wouldn't let her down.

I was looking forward to writing a great story, and to be honest I was even more excited about all the delicious food I was going to buy with the two dollars.

Yum!

Sunday 30th May

I headed straight for Milton's Diner when I
left the apartment this morning and ordered
a plate of waffles with maple syrup, three
doughnuts and a bowl of vanilla ice cream with
marshmallow whip. I've been past the place so
many times and wondered what it would be like
to just stroll in and order what I wanted, and
now I know. It was pretty amazing.

Or at least it was at first. I kept switching back
and forth between the desserts, and I started to
feel full pretty soon. But I forced myself to keep
going in case I never got the chance to eat stuff
like that again.

By the time I'd finished, my stomach was
aching and I could do nothing but wince and
pat my face with a napkin.

I had to remind myself that Dolores had sent
me here to work rather than to eat until I
passed out.

I ignored the pain and focused on my notebook.

In the version I'd told Dolores, a woman has
her jewels stolen on the same day her husband
loses all his money on the stock market. So they
have to get it back from the thieves or they'll

have nothing. They chase after the robbers in their automobile and eventually overpower them.

Dolores said it was a good start, but the chase scene was like too many she'd seen before. She said I needed to replace it with something the audience wasn't expecting.

My first idea was that cowboys could ride in and attack the robbers and then it could be revealed that the whole movie was set in the old West all along. No one would be expecting that, so maybe it would be a twist. But it would also be kind of stupid.

My next thought was that wacky cops in baggy pants could join in the chase, running the wrong way and tripping over each other. And the whole thing could end up with the thieves overbalancing and falling into a lake. Could be good for some laughs, but it might confuse the audience if they're watching a drama that suddenly turns into a comedy.

Nothing I came up with seemed right. I left the diner and trudged home. This was my last chance to impress Dolores and Mr Cheeseman and get a movie made, and I was letting it slip away from me.

It's after ten now, and I still don't have anything to show for it. Here's hoping for a better day tomorrow.

Monday 31st May

I thought of my twist today. But then my life took a twist of its own, and I'm not sure how much my scenario even matters anymore.

I went back to Milton's this morning, and this time I bought just one helping of cinnamon toast instead of piling the whole kitchen into my mouth.

The place was empty except for a guy with a newspaper at the far end, so I was sure I could get away with hogging a table for the whole day.

I couldn't think of a twist, and I found myself staring out of the window. I told myself a good idea wasn't going to just walk past, but then it kind of did.

A young couple with a small child went by. I wondered what would happen if the couple in my story had a little child too, and a whole new version fell into place.

My couple could have a young daughter who likes to stuff things inside her china dolly, and the audience could see this little detail in an early scene. Then the story goes as planned with the woman's jewels getting stolen and the man losing big on the stock market. The couple have to sell all their possessions one by one, and the audience feels sorry for them as they fall into hardship.

Finally, the day comes when they even have to sell their daughter's beloved china doll. The young girl refuses to give it up but her father yanks it away. The dolly falls to the floor and smashes, revealing the jewels. It turns out they weren't stolen at all, but stuffed inside the doll.

Now the couple can sell the jewels and they won't be poor anymore. And they can even buy a new dolly for their daughter.

I was scribbling this down when I noticed something strange about the man with the newspaper. Whenever I looked down at my pad, he would lower his paper. But whenever I looked up, he would raise it again.

I found it a little weird, and I wondered if I should go and work in another diner. But then I told myself not to be such a coward. I had just as much right to be there as he did.

I strode over to the man and asked him if he wanted something. He kept the newspaper up and said nothing.

I grabbed the top of the paper and yanked it down. I meant to question him again, but when I saw who it was, I couldn't speak at all.

It was Dad.

He said he might as well come clean with me if I promised not to tell Mom, Betty and Mabel. It turns out that he was let go from his job on the aqueduct at the end of last month, and since then he's been spending his days queuing at employment agencies and searching through newspaper listings for jobs.

We've been living off his savings, Mabel's salary and my weekly dollar. No wonder he's been worrying about money so much.

He said he didn't want to tell us because we'd be upset and also that he thought he'd get a new job really quickly. But it still hasn't happened. And if he doesn't find work soon, we'll all have to move out to his brother's farm in Wyoming. There are plenty of spare rooms, and we can stay there rent-free if we all help out.

Up to that point, I was feeling sorry for Dad. Now I started feeling sorry for myself.

This is my big chance to get into the movie business. I can't give it up for backbreaking work in the middle of nowhere. I'll spend my whole life haunted by the fantastic career I could have had.

I asked Dad if it would make a difference if I got Mr Cheeseman to double my money. He shook his head and said I'd need to be making

five or six times as much to help cover the costs
of rent and food. He told me to cross my fingers
and hope he got a job in the next few weeks,
otherwise he'd have to tell the truth to Mom
and my sisters and start planning for the move.

Tuesday Ist June

I couldn't bring myself to spend any more
money in the diner now I know how much we
need it. I gave Dad the rest of my coins and
worked from the house today.

Unfortunately, Betty and Mabel realised I
was trying to concentrate so they kept coming
up with chores I was meant to be doing, like
sweeping the floor, dusting the shelves and
washing the dishes.

I had to go to my room and write with one hand so I could keep the other on the handle to stop them coming in. They yelled at me through the walls about how I never help out with housework, but I managed to block them out and finish my scenario.

I think I've got it working, and it will be cheap to make, so Mr Cheeseman should like it too.

I've even included a few bits where the couple worry about money, inspired by our own woes. It's funny. The story has become kind of personal to me now. Maybe Mr Cheeseman wasn't so crazy to think I could use my real-life experiences to write scenarios.

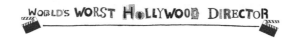

Wednesday 2nd June

Dolores and Alma turned up outside our apartment this morning, just as promised.

Dolores asked if I'd written a good story, and I told her I'd hit it out of the park. She wanted me to read it to her as we drove to the studio, but I said she could hear it at the same time as Mr Cheeseman.

I know this was kind of rude, especially after Dolores had given me that money for the diner, but I knew she'd want to change it, and I really wanted to get it in front of Mr Cheeseman while I was still excited about it.

Besides, I had nothing to lose. I could still end up moving to Wyoming whether Mr Cheeseman liked it or not, so I figured I might as well give it the biggest push I could.

Dolores didn't speak to me much after that. But I didn't have time to make things up with her. I just paced around and read my story over and over, getting ready for my big pitch.

Mr Cheeseman wandered in at noon, flanked once again by two jabbering men in sun visors who were waving wads of paper. He was wearing a bib, sucking on a lobster claw and muttering about how no one would let him enjoy his lunch in peace.

At least he'd eaten something. That was a good start, I thought.

I told Mr Cheeseman I'd written a scenario that only a real person from the street could have come up with. I heard Mortimer muttering 'Give me a break' behind me, but it got Mr Cheeseman's attention. He raised his hand to silence the money men and told me to go ahead.

I cleared my throat and began. I got pretty into it, and was surprised to find my voice breaking up in the bits where the couple worry about money. At one point I even had to wipe away a tear.

Everyone looked at Mr Cheeseman when I'd got
to the end. He finished sucking on the lobster
claw, then tossed it over his shoulder and
grabbed my sheet of notepaper.

He read through it again and said he agreed
that it was written from real experience and
wasn't just another helping of Harvard baloney.
I heard Mortimer sighing behind me.

Then he turned to Dolores and told her we
could go ahead and make the picture. I felt like
jumping up and down and cheering but there
was something I had to do first. I was pleased
my movie was going ahead, but I couldn't stop
thinking about Dad and our money problems.
I figured I'd never get a better opportunity to
press Mr Cheeseman for more cash.

I told Mr Cheeseman that I wanted a dollar
every single day now instead of every week.

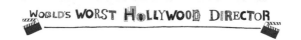

He might want real people like me to write
scenarios, but like a lot of real people, I was
struggling to get by, and the extra money would
make a big difference.

At first he seemed not to have heard me,
turning to one of the sun visor guys and
asking him about one of his bits of paper. But
I repeated my demand, and he said he'd think
about it if the movie came out well.

Okay. So this is good. My movie is going ahead.
And if it's brilliant I might just start making
enough money to help us to stay in Los Angeles.

Chapter 6

Calling the shots

Thursday 3rd June

I think Dolores is really annoyed with me. She's preparing my movie, which Mr Cheeseman is insisting we call *Down to their Last Dollar*. Every time she decides something about sets or props or casting, I jump in with my own opinion straight away.

I know I'm still her assistant, and I don't get a say in how the movie is made just because I wrote it, but my whole future hangs on it coming out well. All it would take would be for Dolores to cast a lousy actor, or Mr Cheeseman to make us include a dance sequence, and I'd be on the way to Wyoming.

Dolores even said she wanted to hand over the measurements to the carpenters herself so our characters didn't wind up living in a doll's house, so I could tell she was still sore with me.

It's fine. She can be snarky if she wants. As long as we end up with a good movie I don't care how we get there.

Sunday 6th June

I told Dad we could get more money if my movie goes well, and he spent all morning asking me about the story. He nodded and said it sounded good, though I could tell he didn't really know what to think. But it made Betty and Mabel jealous that he was taking an interest in my work, so I guess that's something.

Anyhow, we start shooting tomorrow. Here goes.

Monday 7th June

Today didn't get off to a great start. Alma
pulled up outside our apartment as planned,
but Dolores wasn't with her. Apparently she'd
been feeling too dizzy to come along, but she
was going to join us later.

This didn't sound good. There was no way
someone could direct a good movie if they were
dizzy. But we had no choice but to carry on and
get everything ready for Dolores.

I checked the apartment set, which was
thankfully the right size this time. I looked
over the costumes, one smart suit and one
brown dress. Even I couldn't put those on the
wrong actors.

And I greeted the actors May and Clarence
when they showed up. Clarence said he'd get
into character to be ready for when Dolores

arrived. By this he meant sitting on the edge of the stage, closing his eyes and rubbing his forehead like he was concentrating really hard.

There was still no sign of Dolores by noon. I got Wallace to set his camera on the tripod and made the actors rehearse the scene where they discover the jewels have been stolen, just so we were ready to turn over if she showed up.

An hour later, Alma returned, still without Dolores. She said she was too ill to get out of bed, and we'd have to try again tomorrow.

Wallace frowned and said that if Dolores didn't make it in tomorrow, the movie might not happen at all. Mr Cheeseman never moves his schedules around if pictures overrun. He just cancels them.

I watched him pack the tripod away and wondered if I was seeing my big chance fall apart. There was no guarantee that Dolores would recover by tomorrow. And if she didn't, the movie would definitely be dead.

But then I wondered what exactly we were waiting for her to do. The actors looked like they were prepared, the sun was out, and Wallace certainly didn't need any help with filming. Why didn't we just go ahead?

I told everyone to stay where they were because we were going for a take. May and Clarence glanced at each other in confusion. I guess it must have been pretty weird to get ordered around by someone my age, but I didn't care. I just wanted to get the movie done.

Wallace set the camera back up and I called 'Action!' I talked May and Clarence through what they were meant to be feeling as they entered the living room and saw that the jewels were missing.

It wasn't right. Something about their acting seemed a little flat, and I didn't know how to tell them without being rude.

I knew Dolores would be getting better performances out of the actors and I wondered what she had that I didn't. Then I realised what it was. I raced to the office, grabbed her megaphone and we went again.

I said all the same stuff, but now it sounded more official. And it worked much better. You could really believe May and Clarence had just lost their valuable jewels.

I was actually really pleased with this take but I made them do it a few more times because that's what Dolores always does.

Wallace asked me which other shots I wanted to cover and I didn't want to admit I hadn't thought about it. I tried to imagine myself sitting in the nickelodeon. What would I need to see to understand the story? I decided we should film close-ups of May and Clarence in shock, and of the living-room table with and without the jewels on it.

Action!

When all this was covered, we were out of time. Maybe Dolores will insist on doing it all again tomorrow, but I had a lot of fun anyway.

GET REAL

In the very early days of movie-making, directors used long shots, where the whole bodies of the actors could be seen. This is how audiences were used to seeing performers in the theatre, so it seemed like a natural way to make films. But directors such as D.W. Griffith and Edwin S. Porter soon began to work out different ways of telling stories, and one of the most important was the close-up, where the face and shoulders of the actor fill the screen. These shots changed the kind of performances actors gave. It meant they could be more restrained, as audiences would have a better view of their different facial expressions.

Tuesday 8ᵗʰ June

Dolores wasn't in the automobile again this morning and I couldn't stop myself feeling secretly pleased. I'd enjoyed directing the movie, and I was glad I could keep doing it.

Today was a much tougher shoot, though. The actress playing the young girl, who is called Sally, arrived with her parents early on.

At first she was fascinated by the cameras and the stage and went around asking everyone what they were doing. But soon enough she got impatient and started tugging on her mother's sleeve and whining.

I realised you had to work quicker when child actors were around. They have limited concentration, and you have less time to get what you need. I told Wallace to turn over right away and shoot the scene where the girl shoves marbles into her dolly.

First I tried yelling at Sally through the megaphone, but this scared her, and she ran for her mom. Next I went for a different approach, crouching down next to her and talking her through the action. This went a little better, but she couldn't stop glancing up at me to check she was doing it right.

The next time I didn't mention anything about acting. I just said we were going to play a game to see how many marbles she could stuff inside the doll, and this time it worked. She stared down at her toys with perfect concentration, just as I wanted.

150

Stupidly, I made her do two more takes because I thought that's what Dolores would have done. Halfway through the last one, she stamped her feet and said she was sick of making movies.

I pleaded with her to do another scene, but she just cried and threw the doll at me. I thought we might have to stop the filming until Sally

was feeling better, but then I remembered I
didn't have to shoot everything in sequence.
There's a later scene in which Sally is upset
that her dolly has been smashed. It would be a
tough performance to get at any other time, but
if we filmed it now, I knew she wouldn't have to
act at all.

I got Wallace to set up the new shot quickly,
handed Sally the broken dolly prop and we
got a couple of great takes. You might think
directing movies is about having a fancy vision
and being an artistic genius, but so much of it is
about thinking fast and solving problems.

By the time I told everyone to wrap at the end
of the day, I'd totally forgotten I wasn't the
actual director on the movie.

Wednesday 9th June

Okay, I'll admit it. I didn't want Dolores to be in the automobile this morning, but she was. Her eyes were red and she was holding a handkerchief to her nose. She'd had a bout of flu, but said she was up to working again.

She wasn't happy when I told her I'd already started. She said I should have waited, even if it might have meant the movie got cancelled. She said we'd have to start over, reshooting everything again.

I tried not to get mad with her. After all, I'd gone ahead without her permission, so it was no wonder she was being grouchy.

I took a deep breath and calmly suggested she take a look at the footage so far before deciding whether it really needed doing again. She eventually agreed.

We went straight to the projection room when we got to Cheeseman City. I couldn't bear to sit next to Dolores while my precious footage was running, so I waited outside the room and tried to stay calm.

She was in there for half an hour, so she must have watched the rushes two or three times. I couldn't tell if this was a good sign or not.

Dolores stepped out into the light. I promised myself I wouldn't cry if she said she didn't like what I'd done.

She clasped my shoulder and said the footage was so good I should keep on directing the movie. Despite what I'd promised myself, I felt tears running down my cheeks.

Dolores said she'd give me whatever help I wanted, but I'd make the final decisions and get the credit.

I wiped my eyes on my sleeve and hurried back to the set where Wallace, May and Clarence were waiting.

I grabbed the megaphone and announced that I would be continuing as director. Everyone looked at Dolores as if she were going to snatch it out of my hands and announce that I'd gone crazy, but she just nodded.

I think I might have made May and Clarence do a few too many takes to show Dolores how serious I was, because they got really annoyed. But I got the performances I wanted and that's all that counts.

Thursday 10ᵗʰ June

Today Dolores asked if I was thinking of developing any of my scenes in colour, and I told her I hadn't even considered it. I wondered if the scene where the jewels go missing should be tinted red, but I decided it would be dramatic enough without it. I was getting good work from the actors, and with the right editing, audiences would like the movie whether I used gimmicks or not.

GET REAL

We might assume that silent movies were always black and white, but experiments with colour were going on throughout the era. Georges Méliès used a team of artists to colour his films by hand, one frame at a time. A simpler method was tinting, in which dyes were used when developing the film. This could give a single colour to part of a film, as with the red fire scenes in D.W. Griffith's The Birth of a Nation.

Friday 11ᵗʰ June

So that's it. I've just wrapped my first ever movie. Dad asked how it went when I got home. I tried to tell him but Mabel jumped in and yakked about her job instead. Then Betty jumped in and started talking about Ed's job so she didn't feel left out.

But if I could have replied to Dad, I'd have told him I'm pretty pleased. But it's hard to be sure until you get the film back from the laboratory.

Sunday 13*th* June

Okay. So my movie works. I think. I've seen it so many times now I can't really tell.

I spent today editing it in the room at the side of the laboratory. Dolores kept encouraging me to remove extra frames from the beginnings and ends of each scene, and I got worried that it would go by so fast it would be hard to follow.

It seemed fine when we ran it through the projector, though. Not that it matters what I think. Mr Cheeseman is going to watch it tomorrow and he's the one who'll decide whether it's good enough to send out to the theatres.

I just hope he won't be too hungry when he watches it.

Chapter 7
Hollywood ending

Monday 14th June

Mr Cheeseman was meant to watch my movie at nine this morning, but he still hadn't shown up by ten. It was far too hot inside the projection room, so we waited outside. Dolores threw around ideas for her next movie, but I couldn't stop worrying about today.

There was still no sign of him by 11, and I realised we were getting into the pre-lunch hunger zone.

Dolores said she once showed him a serious drama about a gambler when he was hungry, and he insisted that she shoot new scenes in which the family dog performs tricks. He thinks you can't go wrong with performing animals and I got worried he might add some dancing elephants or something into mine.

I asked if we could put the screening back, but she said we might lose our slot forever and the movie would be left to gather dust on the shelf. I thought about my precious can of film turning into a giant fur ball through years of neglect. That would be worse than anything. We'd have to take our chances with Mr Cheeseman, whatever state his stomach was in.

He finally arrived at a quarter after twelve. There was no bib, no lobster claw and no soup stains on his shirt. This was not good. Even worse, I heard his stomach grumble.

A guy wearing a sun visor followed him in, showing him a stack of scary legal documents sent by the patents guys. It seemed like I could hardly have got him at a worse time.

He sat in a chair and stared at the wall while

Dolores ran my movie on the projector. The sun visor guy was still trying to speak, but I gave him a hard shove and told him to zip it while my movie was playing.

At first Mr Cheeseman slouched back and muttered angrily to himself. My movie obviously wasn't taking his mind off his thoughts of food and money.

But when it got to the scene where May and Clarence discover the jewels are missing, he went quiet. When the cops showed up he sat forward and clasped his hands. And when the dolly finally smashed apart to reveal the jewels, he leapt up and yelled that he'd known it all along.

Dolores whispered that she'd never seen him react so well.

The end title appeared and Mr Cheeseman stood up and clasped my shoulder. He said I'd done a great job and we could send the movie out just as it was.

I found myself grinning, but I forced myself to look serious again.

I told Mr Cheeseman I was glad he liked my picture, but I hoped he'd keep his promise to pay me a dollar a day. This made his mysterious deafness kick in and he suddenly wanted to talk to the sun visor guy.

I KNEW IT!

Dolores told Mr Cheeseman to answer me. She said I'd made a great movie and $365 wasn't much to pay for a year of my services. She said Mr Cheeseman had never paid less than fifty dollars for a scenario, so it could work out as a bargain for him.

It sounded pretty good when she put it like that. Maybe I should have asked for even more.

Mr Cheeseman nodded and said I could have the money. Agreeing caused him so much pain he had to get his handkerchief out and mop his brow again.

He stomped out, and I thanked Dolores and asked what I could do to repay her. She told me it was very simple. I had to get back to the office and write a dozen brilliant new scenarios before the end of the day. I knew I shouldn't have asked.

GET REAL

While movie stars could command salaries of a thousand dollars a week, writers often struggled to make a living. In 1915 studios were typically paying between $50 and $100 for original scenarios for single-reel movies. But some writers such as Anita Loos became known for their storytelling skills, and could command much more.

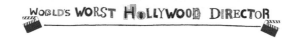

Monday 21ˢᵗ June

I got my first weekly pay of seven dollars today.
I gave five to Dad, and kept two back to take
everyone on a special mystery trip.

Okay, so it wasn't that much of a mystery.
I took Mom, Dad, Mabel, Betty and Ed to a
nickelodeon on Broadway, and none of them
were too surprised when we ended up there.

But there was at least something a little secret
about the outing. I took them to see my movie
Down to Their Last Dollar, but I didn't tell
them it was mine because I wanted to know
what they really thought.

There was a newsreel, a western and a comedy
on first, and they seemed to last forever.
Finally, the Cheeseman Pictures title card
came up and it was time for *Down to Their Last
Dollar*. Dad must have recognised the story,

because he grinned at me, but none of the others realised.

After we'd seen the full programme, I took them all out to Milton's for coffee and desserts, and asked what they thought of the pictures.

They had mixed feelings about the other movies, but everyone enjoyed mine, even Mabel and Betty. Ed actually slapped the table and said it was a real lollapalooza.

I wish Wallace could have been there to record their faces when I told them it was my movie. Betty and Mabel tried to backtrack by saying it was kind of dumb, but it was too late. They'd already admitted they'd liked it.

As I watched my sisters scowling at the remains of their waffles and flushing purple, I realised that I'd managed to get revenge after all. And I didn't need to put insects in their beds or tie their shoelaces together. I just had to do something brilliant that they could never have done.

Friday 2nd July

I've been too busy to write this journal for the
last two weeks. I wish I could say it's because
I've been making movies, but all I've really been
doing is talking to journalists.

It all started with one of Mr Cheeseman's sun
visor guys. He said that instead of paying to
advertise my movie in the *Los Angeles Times*,
we should get them to run a story about me
instead. After all, they'd never released a movie
by someone as young as me before. Maybe there
could be some publicity in it?

There was. A journalist came to interview
me and ran an article about 'Little Miss
Megaphone'. The story spread to other
California newspapers, and then across
the country.

Every day journalists came to talk to me. Some of them wanted to meet me at home to get a fresh angle. One of them, a fast-talking man from the *Daily Herald*, even interviewed and photographed Betty and Mabel. I smirked the next day when they saw their tiny photographs underneath the huge one of me.

Great though all this coverage has been for Cheeseman Pictures, I'm getting tired of being a publicity stunt now and I want to get back to making movies.

Today I wrote a scenario about a young girl who wants to be a ballerina, and she's really talented even though her two horrible sisters are mean to her. Then she finds out her Dad has secretly lost his job and this puts pressure on her to win a dancing contest with a thousand-dollar prize.

I thought I'd better check Dad was okay with it before showing it to Dolores, in case he thought it was about him, which I guess it kind of is.

He said he didn't mind, then gave me some good news of his own. He's found a new job at last, helping to build a new streetcar line. So we can definitely stay in Los Angeles.

It means I can keep more of the money I'm earning, though I doubt Dolores will ever give me any time off to spend it.

I don't really mind. I'd rather be making movies than shopping, anyway. I know some people look down on moving pictures, but they're still pretty new when you think about it. Other ways of telling stories, like plays and poems and novels, have been around for hundreds of years. But movies have only been around for

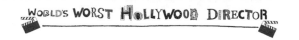

a couple of decades. Who can say what they'll be like twenty years from now? Or fifty? Or a hundred?

I have no idea. But I bet they'll be just as popular, maybe even more so. And I really hope I can keep working in them. Making movies is really hard, but it's also good fun and I want to do it forever.

I don't think I'll be able to keep this journal up, though. I won't have time. So I'm going to finish it right now like it was one of my movies:

The End

The Birth of Hollywood

Movies work through a simple magic trick. When our brains see a quick series of still images, we interpret them as moving continuously. Movies take advantage of this illusion to give us hours of entertainment and make millions of dollars.

With the beginning of photography in the nineteenth century, lots of inventors were looking for ways to record and show images in motion. In 1888, French inventor Louis Le Prince created a camera that could record moving images. He filmed short scenes with it in Leeds, England.

In 1893, Thomas Edison presented the Kinetoscope, a large box which showed short clips to one person at a time. Viewers could watch things such as blacksmiths working, a woman dancing and a man sneezing. They might not sound like much, but for a while they were the greatest films of all time.

In 1895, the Lumière Brothers used their cinematograph to project moving images. Their films included workers leaving a factory and a man getting sprayed in the face by a hosepipe, thought to be the first film comedy. So next time you spray your little brother in the face with water, you can say you're paying tribute to film history.

Over the next few years, brilliant filmmakers transformed moving pictures from a fun novelty to an exciting new way of telling stories. A French magician called Georges Méliès pioneered special effects. His short films such as *A Trip to the Moon* can be found on YouTube and are still fascinating to watch.

An American director called Edwin S. Porter found new ways of moving the camera and editing scenes together in films like *The Great Train Robbery*.

And a stage actor called D.W. Griffith switched to making movies and became the most successful director of the era. Before Hitchcock, Kubrick and Spielberg, Griffith was the movie director whose name was known by the general public.

American filmmakers were initially based in places like New York and Chicago, but they eventually moved out to Hollywood in Los Angeles. Hollywood had year-round sunshine, perfect for filming outdoors, and a great variety of locations within easy reach. It was also far away from Thomas Edison and the patents company, who were known to violently disrupt movie-makers who hadn't paid their licensing fees.

At first most films were just one reel long, about 10 to 16 minutes. But moviemakers soon expanded them into 'feature films', which could run to over two hours. An Australian film from 1906 called *The Story of the Kelly Gang* is credited as the first feature film, and there were many other popular examples over the next few years, such as *Quo Vadis?*

from Italy and *The Loves of Queen Elizabeth*
from France.

The movie that made features a true
sensation was D.W. Griffith's *The Birth
of a Nation* in 1915. An epic story of the
American Civil War that ran for around
three hours, it made millions of dollars and
changed the expectations of moviegoers.
But it was also accused of racism and
inspiring the hate group The Ku Klux
Klan to re-form.

Hollywood produced hundreds of classic
feature-length movies over the next few
years. Charlie Chaplin mixed comedy
with drama in *The Kid* (1921). Buster
Keaton brought jaw-dropping action to the
slapstick genre in *The General* (1926).

And Lon Chaney terrified audiences in the early horror movie *The Phantom of the Opera* (1925).

It was a great time for movies, but another big change was on the way. Inventors had been looking for ways to combine sound with moving pictures since the late 19th century. By the middle of the 1920s the technology to match recorded sound with pictures was in place. The first big hit to take advantage of this was *The Jazz Singer* in 1927.

The silent movie era was over, and the 'talkies' had arrived.

Timeline

1888

Louis Le Prince makes a short film in Leeds called *Roundhay Garden Scene*. And it really is short, clocking in at just over 2 seconds.

1893

Thomas Edison unveils the Kinetoscope in Brooklyn, USA. The first film to be shown is called *Blacksmith Scene*.

1895

The Lumière brothers hold the first public screening with their cinematograph machine. It includes films such as *Workers Leaving the Lumière Factory*, which lasts for a whopping 46 seconds.

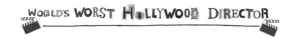

Timeline

1896

The Lumière brothers unveil their film *The Arrival of a Train at La Ciotat Station*. According to popular myth, the audience thought a real train was coming towards them and leapt out of their seats. But even the first movie audiences would have known they were watching a fun illusion.

1902

Georges Méliès creates his fantasy film *A Trip to the Moon*. He produces both black-and-white and hand-painted colour prints of the movie.

1903

Edwin S. Porter's landmark Western *The Great Train Robbery* is shown. It ends with a bandit firing a gun at the camera, a shot that subsequently inspired both Martin Scorsese and the James Bond intro.

Timeline

1905

A movie theatre charging five cents admission opens in a storefront in Pittsburgh, USA. It's called the 'Nickelodeon'. The idea and name are quickly copied by hundreds of others, and nickelodeons soon appear all over the USA.

1910

Director D.W. Griffith travels to Los Angeles to make a few movies. He films *In Old California* in a small village to the north called Hollywood. Word spreads about this great location and within a few years much of the American movie business relocates there.

1914

Charlie Chaplin makes his movie debut. He soon becomes one of the richest and best-known people in the world.

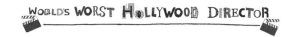

Timeline

1915
D.W. Griffith's *The Birth of a Nation* is released. It is extremely controversial, but makes a lot of money, and proves there is a huge audience for feature-length movies.

1919
Charlie Chaplin, D.W. Griffith, Mary Pickford and Douglas Fairbanks form a studio called United Artists. They believe that creative people should have more control over their own work.

1927
The Jazz Singer is a smash hit, heralding the era of movies with sound, known as 'talkies'.

Early Cinema Hall of Fame

Charlie Chaplin (1889–1977)

British comedian who used the new medium of film to become the most famous person in the world. His 'Little Tramp' character, complete with baggy pants, walking cane, bowler hat and moustache, is still an icon of cinema 100 years after it was created. A complicated genius, Chaplin was one of the major figures of the 20th century.

D.W. Griffith (1875–1948)

The most successful director of the early Hollywood era. He developed some of the basic ways of telling stories on film, drew on his background as an actor to get believable performances from his stars, and helped to drive the switch from short films to feature-length ones.

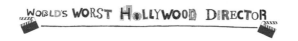
Early Cinema Hall of Fame

Thomas Edison (1847–1931)
William Kennedy Dickson (1860–1935)

Thomas Edison was one of the greatest inventors who ever lived, but he sometimes gets the credit for devices that were actually created by his team in Menlo Park, New Jersey. So he's sharing space in this hall of fame with his assistant William Kennedy Dickson. Together they developed the kinetoscope, which allowed one person at a time to watch very short movies.

Douglas Fairbanks (1883–1939)

One of the first big movie stars, Douglas Fairbanks was famous for starring in action-packed adventure stories such as *Robin Hood*, *The Thief of Bagdad* and *The Mark of Zorro*. These kinds of films were called 'swashbucklers'.

187

Early Cinema Hall of Fame

Carl Laemmle (1867–1939)

The founder of Universal Studios and one of the first great 'movie moguls'. Laemmle moved to America from Germany in the late 19th century and got involved with the movie business through owning nickelodeons. He was one of the original movie bosses to promote his actors as stars and he had a talent for publicity. For example, he once spread the rumour that Florence Lawrence had died in a streetcar crash and then took out newspaper ads to deny it.

Yum!

Early Cinema Hall of Fame

Florence Lawrence (1886–1938)

Canadian actress who is sometimes called 'the first movie star'. Her short films for the Biograph Company earned her an army of fans. But this was in the days before actors were credited, so she was simply called 'the Biograph Girl'. Her real name became known to the public when she left Biograph to work with Carl Laemmle.

August Lumière (1862–1954)
Louis Lumière (1864–1948)

The Lumière brothers were French inventors who came up with the cinematograph, which worked as both a film camera and a projector. This meant a large audience could view a film at the same time, so the machine is said to mark the true birth of cinema. Their surname means 'light', oddly enough.

Early Cinema Hall of Fame

Georges Méliès (1861–1938)

French magician who pioneered the art of special effects. He used simple tricks like running film through a camera twice to create seemingly impossible images. His 'in-camera' effects showed other movie-makers what was possible in cinema.

Mary Pickford (1892–1979)

Canadian actress who became one of the first big Hollywood stars. Originally a stage performer, she was discovered by D.W. Griffith and crossed over into movies. Some of her fellow stage actors thought she was mad to devote herself to a fad like cinema, but in a few years she was one of the most famous women in the world and known as 'America's Sweetheart'. She went on to co-found the film studio United Artists.

Early Cinema Hall of Fame

Edwin S. Porter (1870–1941)

American cinematographer and director whose short films pioneered some of the ways stories could be told on film. His 1903 movie *The Great Train Robbery* featured clever editing and camera work, and was shot on location rather than in a studio. It's been called the first action movie, so he's the one to blame for all those films where men in vests run away from explosions.

Lois Weber (1879–1939)

American director who was one of the most important early movie-makers. She made hundreds of short films, including *Suspense* in 1913, which made early use of the split-screen technique to show three different images at once. In 1914, she became the first American woman to direct a feature film with *The Merchant of Venice*.

Glossary

Cinematograph
A machine that could create and project movies, invented by the Lumière brothers.

Close-up
A type of movie shot in which something, for example the face of an actor or an object, fills most of the frame.

Editing
The process of selecting, ordering and trimming footage into a finished movie.

Kinetoscope
A device invented by Thomas Edison and William Kennedy Dickson that allowed one person at a time to watch movies.

Mogul
A powerful and important person, usually someone who works in the movie industry.

Nickelodeon
A small movie theatre, often based in a storefront, that charged five cents admission.

Glossary

Patent
The legal right to make or sell an invention, such as, for example, the movie camera.

Photoplay
An old term for movies and also the name of a popular magazine that was published between 1911 and 1980.

Reel
A term used in early moviemaking to refer to 1,000 feet of 35-millimetre film, which would run for between 10 and 16 minutes.

Rushes
The raw footage from a day of filming.

Glossary

Scenario
A written outline of a movie's story.

Studio
A company that produces movies.

Talkie
A film with speech, sound and music. Talkies took over from silent movies in the late 1920s.

Take
A version of a scene from a particular camera set-up. Some directors such as Stanley Kubrick were famous for recording lots of different takes of the same scenes.

Tinting
The use of dye in the developing process to give movie scenes a single colour.

Title
A short piece of text that appears on screen. In silent movies, they were used to reveal the background to the story and the characters' dialogue.

Wrap
A term used when filming is complete, either for the day or for an entire movie.

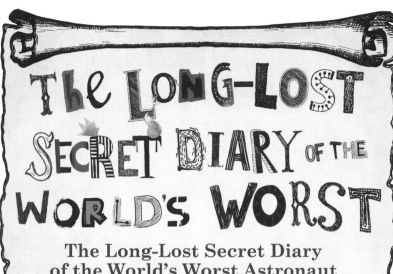

THE LONG-LOST SECRET DIARY OF THE WORLD'S WORST

**The Long-Lost Secret Diary
of the World's Worst Astronaut**
Chosen for the 2019 Summer
Reading Challenge.

**The Long-Lost Secret Diary
of the World's Worst Pirate**
Shortlisted for the
Lancashire School Library Service
Fantastic Book Awards (FBA) 2017–18.

*'Although easy to read, the vocabulary
is great and the plot lines engaging –
excellent reads for developing readers.'*
Library Girl and Book Boy Blog

PB ISBN: 978-1-912233-19-9

PB ISBN: 978-1-912233-20-5

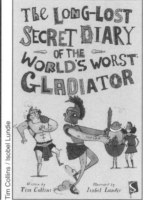

PB ISBN: 978-1-912537-26-6

PB ISBN: 978-1-912006-67-0

PB ISBN: 978-1-912006-66-3

PB ISBN: 978-1-912537-44-0

PB ISBN: 978-1-912904-23-5

A selected list of Scribo titles

The prices shown below are correct at the time of going to press. However, The Salariya Book Company reserves the right to show new retail prices on covers, which may differ from those previously advertised.

Gladiator School by Dan Scott

1 Blood Oath	978-1-908177-48-3	£6.99
2 Blood & Fire	978-1-908973-60-3	£6.99
3 Blood & Sand	978-1-909645-16-5	£6.99
4 Blood Vengeance	978-1-909645-62-2	£6.99
5 Blood & Thunder	978-1-910184-20-2	£6.99
6 Blood Justice	978-1-910184-43-1	£6.99

Shivers by John Townsend

1 Ghost Stories	978-1-912233-52-6	£6.99
2 Pirate Stories	978-1-912233-51-9	£6.99

Scarlet Hood by Mark Evans

	978-1-912233-34-2	£7.99

Ballet School by Fiona Macdonald
1. Peter & The Wolf   978-1-911242-37-6   £6.99
2. Samira's Garden   978-1-912006-62-5   £6.99

The Curse of the Speckled Monster
   by John Townsend
1 Graverobbers & Gallows   978-1-912233-32-8 £6.99
2 The Twist of the Hangman 978-1-912233-33-5 £6.99

The Shakespeare Plot by Alex Woolf
1 Assassin's Code   978-1-911242-38-3   £9.99
2 The Dark Forest   978-1-912006-95-3   £9.99
3 The Powder Treason   978-1-912006-33-5   £9.99

Visit our website at:

www.salariya.com

All Scribo and Salariya Book Company titles can be
ordered from your local bookshop, or by post from:

The Salariya Book Co. Ltd,
25 Marlborough Place
Brighton
BN1 1UB